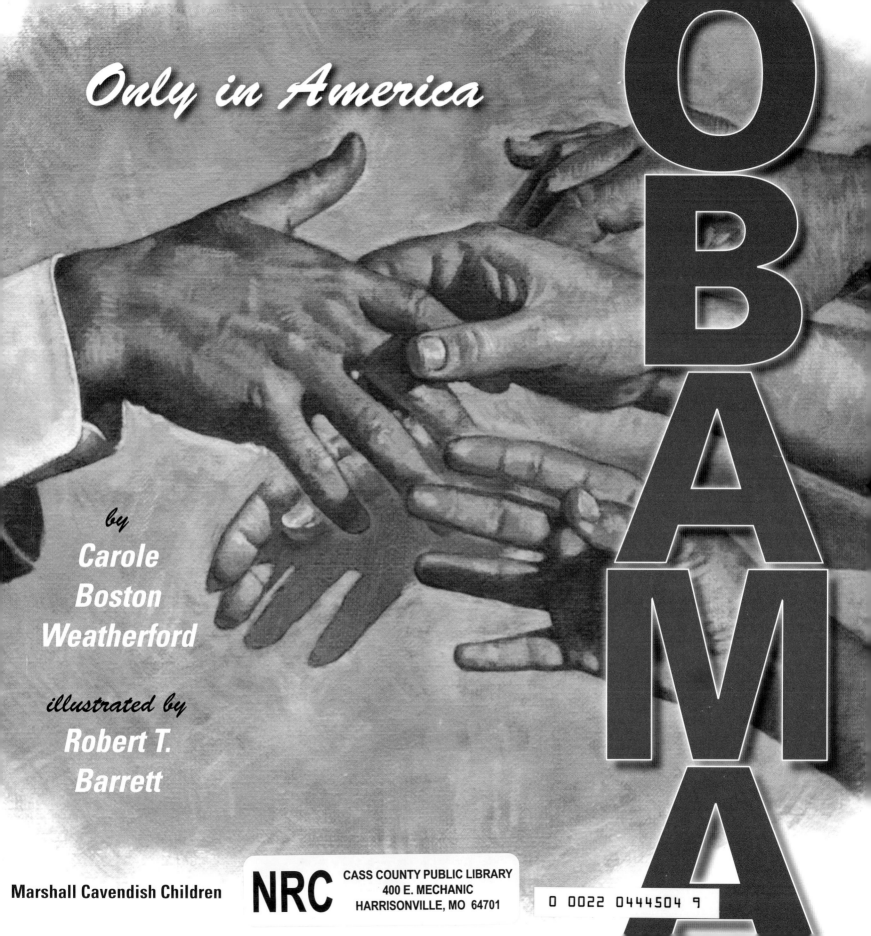

Only in America

OBAMA

by
Carole Boston Weatherford

illustrated by
Robert T. Barrett

Marshall Cavendish Children

Marshall Cavendish Corporation, 99 White Plains Road, Tarrytown, NY 10591
www.marshallcavendish.us/kids

Library of Congress Cataloging-in-Publication Data
Weatherford, Carole Boston, 1956-
Obama : only in America / by Carole Boston Weatherford ; illustrated by Robert T. Barrett. — 1st ed.
p. cm.
ISBN 978-0-7614-5641-4
1. Obama, Barack—Juvenile literature. 2. Presidents—United States—Biography—Juvenile literature.
3. Racially mixed people—United States—Biography—Juvenile literature. I. Barrett, Robert, 1949- ill. II. Title.
E908.W43 2010
973.932092—dc22
[B]
2009006338

The illustrations are rendered in oil on canvas.

Book design by Anahid Hamparian

Editor: Margery Cuyler
Printed in Malaysia (T)
First edition
1 3 5 6 4 2

Marshall Cavendish
Children

To Caresse and Jeffery, whose first votes made history:
The world is yours to change.

—C.B.W.

For Vicki and the kids

—R.T.B.

" . . . for as long as I live,
I will never forget that in no other country on Earth
is my story even possible."

from "A More Perfect Union," Philadelphia, PA, March 18, 2008

The son of a Kenyan goat herder
and a daughter of Kansas
married and had a baby—
born the fourth day of August 1961
in the fiftieth state, Hawaii.
They named him Barack—
meaning "blessed" in Swahili—
and they called him Barry.

"My parents shared not only an improbable love; they shared an abiding faith in the possibilities of this nation."

from "Keynote Address" at the 2004 Democratic National Convention, Boston, MA, July 27, 2004

He was just two when his parents split.
His mother, Ann, soon remarried.
They moved with her new husband,
Lolo, to Jakarta, Indonesia. There,
beggars knocked on the door
and crocodiles sunned in the yard.
Barry played with his pet monkey,
ate snake meat and roasted grasshoppers,
and learned to box from Lolo.

"I may be skinny but I'm tough too."

from a campaign speech in College Park, MD, February 11, 2008

Barry now had a baby sister, Maya.
School days, their mother woke him
before sunrise to give him English lessons.
When he griped, she'd say,
"This is no picnic for me either, Buster!"
She wanted the best education for him
even if it meant sending her ten-year-old son
back to Honolulu to live with her parents—
the grandparents he barely remembered.

Gramps had fought in World War II
and sold furniture for a living.
His grandmother Toot had risen
from secretary to bank vice president
and still rode the bus to work.

" . . . the American dream isn't something that
happens to you—it's something you strive for and
work for and seize with your own two hands."

remarks to the Urban League, Orlando, FL, August 2, 2008

Gramps and Toot were proud as could be
when Barry got into Punahou Academy.
They poured heart and soul into him.
He and Gramps greeted Apollo astronauts
who'd been to the moon and splashed down
in the Pacific. Barry waved a flag for those heroes.
It was a great time to be American.

" . . . we must pledge once more to march into the future."

from "The American Promise," Democratic National Convention,
Denver, CO, August 28, 2008

When Barry was ten, his father visited.
He brought carvings from Kenya—
a lion, an elephant, and a drummer—
took Barry to a jazz concert, and gave him
his first basketball for Christmas.
The day Barack Sr. left for Kenya,
he and Barry danced to African records.
They'd spent a month together
and would never meet again.

"For most of my life I knew him only through the letters he sent and the stories my mother and grandparents told."

from "Strengthening Families in a New Economy,"
Spartanburg, SC, June 15, 2007

Without his father around,
Barry had to raise himself to be a black man.
He turned to TV, radio, and movies,
and Gramps's poker buddy Frank,
who wrote poetry and drank from jelly jars.
Barry learned to dance from *Soul Train*
and to shoot hoops at the playground.
To him, the all-black starting five
on UH's winning basketball team were warriors.

Barry was one of only three blacks in his school.
Once, a classmate called him a "coon."
That boy got a bloody nose.
Sometimes Barry scoffed about "white folks."
Then the memory of his mother's smile
would remind him that kindness is color blind.
Still, Barry was at odds with himself.

*" . . . beneath all the differences of race and region, faith
and station, we are one people."*

from "Announcement Speech for President," Springfield, IL, February 10, 2007

In high school, Barry shot hoops,
worked at a burger chain, drove Gramps's old
Ford Granada, and tried to lose self-doubt in drink and drugs.
He walked two worlds—black and white—
and wanted more than anything
to belong someplace. But where?
He was at ease on the basketball court,
where skin color mattered less
than whether he scored.
His jump shot earned him the nickname
Barry O'Bomber.

"I want to win. . . ."

from "Announcement Speech for President,"
Springfield, IL, February 10, 2007

In secret, he read books by black writers—
James Baldwin, Ralph Ellison,
Langston Hughes, Richard Wright,
and W. E. B. DuBois—for a road map
to self-respect. But only Malcolm X's story
spoke to him. From gangster to prisoner,
from tough-talking minister to humanitarian,
Malcolm had remade himself.
Perhaps Barry could do the same
if he'd use the brain he was born with.
But he had to wake up first.

Back from her fieldwork overseas,
his mother sounded the alarm.
She marched into Barry's room,
called him a loafer, and ordered him
to get busy applying to colleges.

"That's the promise of education in America—that no matter what we look like or where we come from or who our parents are, each of us should have the opportunity to fulfill our God-given potential."

from 80th Convention of the American Federation of Teachers, Chicago, IL, July 13, 2008

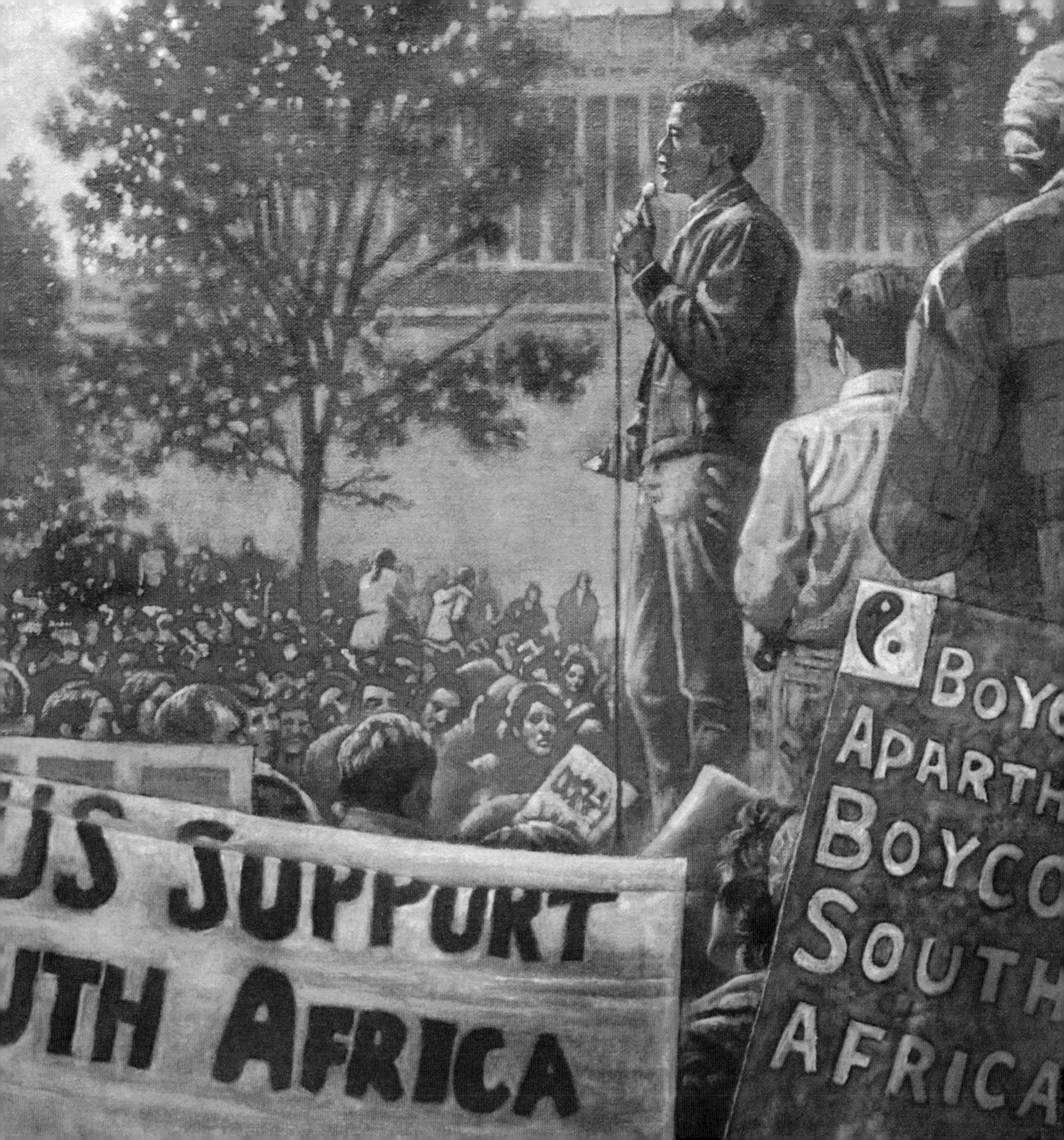
US SUPPORT
UTH AFRICA
BOYC
APARTH
BOYCO
SOUTH
AFRICA

He went to Occidental College in Los Angeles.
There, he grew into his given name, Barack,
and first sensed his calling: to speak out
against injustice and for those without a voice.
At a campus protest rally, his brief speech
brought cheers and applause: Tell it like it is!
For a few minutes, the power of words swept him up.
He saw the need to change the world.
But he still struggled with a big question:
Where did he belong?

*"There is not a black America and white America and Latino
America and Asian America; there's the United States of America."*

from "Keynote Address at the 2004 Democratic National Convention,"
Boston, MA, July 27, 2004

Letters from his father in Kenya gave no answers.
Nor did entering Columbia University
in New York. He buckled down,
studied hard, stopped getting high,
and ran three miles a day. He saw a city
divided by differences: between rich
and poor and whites and people of color.
Barack was sure of one thing:
he wanted to be a bridge.

*"What is called for . . . is that we do unto others
as we would have them do unto us."*

from "A More Perfect Union," Philadelphia, PA, March 18, 2008

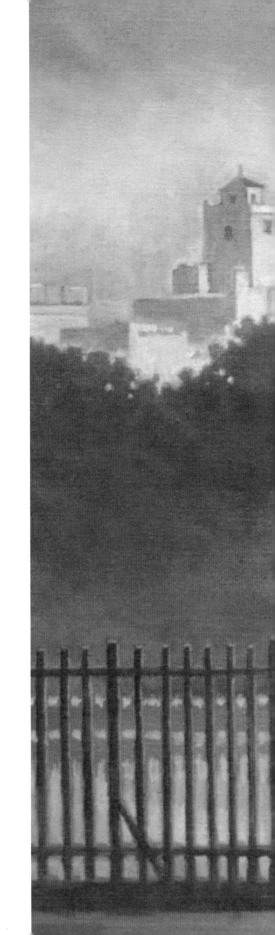

But he still yearned to know his African roots,
to visit Kenya. Before he could, a car wreck
took his father's life. A year later, Barry
saw his father in a dream and awoke in tears.
Other nights, fuzzy gray images of marches,
sit-ins, and voter registration drives
flashed through his mind like prayers.
In no time, Barack had graduated from college.

*"We know the difference we can make when we
work together to open the doors of opportunity
wide enough for everyone to walk through."*

remarks to the Urban League, Orlando, FL, August 2, 2008

Hard as he tried, he could not find
a community-organizing job.
He worked in business instead
and soon had his own office, secretary,
and bank account. But he walked away
from that job to serve the community.
Before long, Barack was hungry—and broke.
But his life's work had begun.

*" . . . brick by brick, calloused hand by calloused
hand, people who love this country can change it."*

remarks to the 99th Annual Convention of the NAACP,
Cincinnati, OH, July 14, 2008

In Chicago, he found a job and a mission:
to inspire people to fight for themselves.
In meetings on the city's South Side,
he listened to residents and received
a priceless education. Community leaders
opened their homes and hearts, and became
like family to Barack. Then, his half sister Auma
visited from Kenya—a branch from his roots.

"That work taught me a fundamental truth that has guided me to this day: that change doesn't come from the top down, it comes from the bottom up."

remarks to the Urban League, Orlando, FL, August 2, 2008

The more he heard of residents' hopes
and hardships, the more he wanted to lift them up.
Knowing he could do more good as a lawyer,
he applied to law school and got into Harvard.
But first he went to Kenya to face his history,
meet his family, and make himself whole.

In his father's homeland, no one asked
how to spell his name or said it wrong.
Barack saw Masai women in the marketplace
and went on safari with Auma.
Aunts, uncles, half sisters and brothers,
cousins, and his grandmother welcomed him
like a long lost son, greeting him
with handshakes and hugs. They fed him
goat curry and collards and stories
about his father, whom he'd hardly known.
Barack found that his namesake
was not a god—just a man.
At his father's grave, Barack wept.

"... *what drew my father to America's shores—*
is a set of ideals that speak to aspirations shared by all people."

from "A World that Stands as One," Berlin, Germany, July 24, 2008

Back home, he entered law school,
studied into the wee hours in dusky libraries,
learned the Constitution inside out, and landed
a summer job with a big Chicago law firm.
He met Michelle, his future wife,
and bought her ice cream on their first date.

Barack became the first African American
elected president of *Harvard Law Review*,
the nation's top law journal.
His name was in *The New York Times*.
After law school he could have worked
for a Supreme Court justice or a top law firm.
Committed to lifting people up,
he became a civil rights lawyer
and a law professor. And he married Michelle.

" . . . we may have different stories, but we hold common hopes."

from "A World that Stands as One," Berlin, Germany, July 24, 2008

By 1996 Barack could no longer deny
his political ambitions. He won election
to the Illinois state senate. In Springfield,
the state capital, he followed Lincoln's footsteps,
proving himself bill by bill. A quick study,
he set his sights on Washington too soon
and lost his bid for Congress.
A father now, he would learn patience
from daughters Malia and Sasha
and see the world through new eyes.

"What gives me the most hope is the next generation."

from "A More Perfect Union," Philadelphia, PA, March 18, 2008

State Senator Obama returned to Springfield,
worked even harder, spoke out
against the war that was brewing,
and ran for the United States Senate.
He was tapped to keynote the 2004
Democratic National Convention.
Thrust onto the national stage, he spoke
like a poet of a better America—a nation
not divided by race or class or religion
but united around shared hopes and dreams.

*"We all want to move in the same direction—
towards a better future for our children and grandchildren."*

from "A More Perfect Union," Philadelphia, PA, March 18, 2008

After that soaring speech, Obama's star
burned brighter than ever. He won by a landslide
and became only the third black man
elected U.S. senator since Reconstruction.
Even as he was sworn in, there were whispers
that he could one day be president.
And while he made laws on Capitol Hill,
those whispers became chants: *Obama! Obama!*
It was clear: he would not choose the time to run
for president; time had already chosen him.

"This moment—this election—is our chance to keep, in the twenty-first century, America's promise alive."

from "The American Promise," Democratic National Convention, Denver, CO, August 28, 2008

So on a blustery February day, he returned
to Springfield and stood in the shadow of Lincoln,
that other lanky lawmaker from Illinois.
Barack Obama stood in sixteen-degree cold
and, with his family beside him, announced
that he would seek the highest office in the land.

". . . the time is now to shake off our slumber,
and slough off our fear, and make good on the debt
we owe past and future generations."

from "Announcement Speech for President," Springfield, IL, February 10, 2007

But even he wondered if a skinny black guy
with big ears and a funny name could win.
After all, he faced seven opponents, including Senator
Hillary Clinton, the former First Lady.
She would be tough to beat.
But as he crisscrossed the country, he drew crowds
larger than any candidate before him.
He shook hands, kissed babies, hugged
mothers who had lost sons to war, and spoke
from the heart to citizens, young and old,
hungry for change. Before long he bore
the dreams of millions—not to finally send
an African American to the White House
but to send children to college, to own homes,
to afford doctors' care, to cure America's ills,
to save the planet, and to know peace.

*"...The greatest gift we can pass on to our children
is the gift of hope."*

remarks at Apostolic Church of God, Chicago, IL, June 15, 2008

Obama won the Democratic Party's nomination,
visited soldiers in Iraq and leaders in Europe,
and spoke to hundreds of thousands
in the once-divided city of Berlin.
Overseas, he was like a rock star.
The world moved to his drumbeat.

". . . there is no challenge too great for a world that stands as one."

from "A World that Stands as One," Berlin, Germany, July 24, 2008

He had a keen mind, a cool head, and a gift for speaking.
He would need all that and more to defeat
longtime senator John McCain, a war hero.
On the campaign trail, Obama shot hoops to unwind.
And when the two men faced off in debates,
Obama made it plain to his fellow Americans:
This election is not about me; it's about you.

Citizens heard their highest hopes in his voice
and saw their fondest dreams in his face.
He mirrored the best of all of us, and the good in all of us.
More than a poet, he was a candle in the darkness.
Neither his grandmother's passing nor autumn rain
nor his own tears could douse the flame.
Obama's faith in America's future glowed—
so brightly that voters believed
he would not only keep his word,
but also renew America's promise.
He was a beacon, our best hope for a new day.
And we the people chose hope.

*". . . few obstacles can withstand the power of millions
of voices calling for change."*

from "Announcement Speech for President," Springfield, IL, February 10, 2007

"The time has come to reaffirm our enduring spirit; to choose our better history; to carry forward that previous gift, that noble idea passed on from generation to generation: the god-given promise that all are equal, all are free, and all deserve a chance to pursue their full measure of happiness."

from "Inaugural Address," January 21, 2009

AMERICAN BAPTISM *

by Carole Boston Weatherford

An ancestral spring rises in us
as we scale a mountain to cast this vote;
a stream dammed up beyond possibility,
now liquid and electric in our veins.
A river of tears greets the news
that's been generations coming,
and we wonder, "Is this like Jubilee?"

The movement cradled by a dream
is now a wave. We are surfing toward
the horizon when the tide of tomorrow
carries millions more like us—multitudes
cresting in a sea of hope and humanity,
a second coming—to a hallowed shore.
As Lincoln overlooks the reflecting Pool,
we know that we stand on promises.

Ghosts wade into the Mississippi.
Surely, America has been baptized.

* written by the author to commemorate Barack Obama's election to the presidency of the United States